WHERE HEAT LOOMS

ANDRÉ DU BOUCHET

Where Heat Looms

*Translated from the French
with an Essay by
David Mus*

SUN & MOON PRESS
LOS ANGELES • 1996

Sun & Moon Press
A Program of The Contemporary Arts Educational Project, Inc.
a nonprofit corporation
6026 Wilshire Boulevard, Los Angeles, California 90036

This edition first published in 1996 by Sun & Moon Press
10 9 8 7 6 5 4 3 2 1
FIRST ENGLISH LANGUAGE EDITION 1996

©1961 by Mercure de France
English language translation ©1996 by David Mus
"Translating André du Bouchet" ©1996 by David Mus
Published originally in French as *Dans la chaleur vacante*, 1961.
Reprinted by permission Mercure de France
Biographical material ©1996 by Sun & Moon Press

This book was made possible, in part, through an operational grant from the
Andrew W. Mellon Foundation and through contributions to
The Contemporary Arts Educational Project, Inc.,
a nonprofit corporation

Cover: Alberto Giacometti, *André du Bouchet* (etching, 1961)
Design: Katie Messborn
Typography: Guy Bennett

LIBRARY OF CONGRESS CATALOGING IN PUBLICATION DATA
du Bouchet, André
Where Heat Looms
p. cm—(Sun & Moon Classics: 87)
ISBN: 1-55713-238-0
I. Title. II. Series. III. Translator
811'. 54—dc20

Printed in the United States of America on acid-free paper.

Contents

WHERE HEAT LOOMS

Within the Scythe's Reach

I

Such dryness as opens up day, at
      daybreak.

To the ends, while the storm swings end
                           to end, to and fro.

On roads keeping dry through rain.

The huge earth pours, nothing is lost.

Sky rip, and solid ground underfoot.

I lend life to roads' linkage.

II

Mountain, earth drunk, by daylight failing, the wall

won't budge.

Mountain like
a flaw in wind

frozen solid.

Bright haze skimming the road,
lighting up paper surfaces.

Not to speak before such sky, torn

day surging

comes down

to a house, given, for breathing.

I've seen daylight stricken where the wall is

    still in place.

III

Sunup flays the shins.

Watch, wait, the while, shutters drawn, in
the one-room white.

What whitens shows up late.

        I run straight into day's swirl.

The Basics

1

Strength

or a mighty fit of coughing

unbelievable freeze.

2

Keep level, inches away
from its brow, in the unsteady, crippling blaze.

As a tree gives in cold, the wall crossed over
yields, as well, the true picture.

Hands the same winds of an evening,
                            stopped, on the road,

            burn.

3

First blank stammering

such froth

look here
face all stone-shot

alongside each wheel

straws' hollow

crackle

near the light source.

4

Fire

such fire
as kindles again
within earth closed up

I shut off the white door

a breath
uttered by the field

light

reins.

5

At worst,

      storm put to sleep against a wall. Same
mountain, this pebble burying the mountain.

Useless road, night fallen, strewn with pockets of
black, dark land increasing.

I have built up one summer of sundry days, beyond
hands' strength, beyond earth, done, gone.

Harsh Reach

Given fire, that its redhot spikes run right through dark,
   a woman will stay up watching.

Dust on ice, glacial, through it I glimpse sky, frozen,
         crossed, later, nighttime, on
choppy ground. Day will
                        spade up the chest.

Before my path can stray too far over the face of the
stones.

Groundswell, crowned by last air, look, layer unseen,
untrod.

Here is the earth you cross far from any road and freed

from roads.

New Love

Come so far,

        sleeping on, that I think on sleep.

I must think on sleep.

    Plowland,

        its keen edge that I should see, hear,

the billowing blade.

Pillow,

    to the ear, ice sheet, missing the head.

        This morning,

            reft us

far off upright.

If I could only set out without breathing, put it that
like air itself I would take roads' own shimmer.

                              Wide
open, the house will keep us no further from
great roads' face,

                    our rumpled bed.

Deep Freeze

1

Blast

great freeze

mask

in homeless

motion

its stone

or summit

wind.

2

As doorway, a blank look.

3

Where, over the same earth packed down, I keep right on
burning, air squeezing us to death, we cannot begin to
make out the wall. I take up all at once the vacant
space ahead, ahead

of you.

4

Second turning, the vague blinding wave of is it an
icefield, air in snatches.

5

I am fed on fire from stones.

I deny myself

there is a hand

outstretched

straining

in midair

you get its look

as if you took it from me

our features everywhere
break out.

Slippage

Shadows,

            briefer, shrunken, now heat, outside, stands

in place of fire. Nothing keeps us apart from what

heats. On the ground of its hearth and home where I,

                                  ex-

hausted,

            make for these cold walls.

Blank Before White

Until sun's blank tint white, come as close as your own

hand, I

                  rush on unquenched.

Through impenetrable daylight, on such a road, everything is
still falling
         and bursting down to the point annealing
    dark wells up.

The open road remains for us unbroken by the heat which
sends us off
         reflective. Unless you pull up short of
such heat, not caring. The road runs on ahead where I
sink, down, darkened, with the wind.

Setting out not knowing

                                along what roads our breath is,
again, to be withdrawn. Daylight, falling even, all
about, attends us.

My hand, withdrawn already, and renewing, daily strikes
scarcely through the drought,

            flaming.

Welkin

Let room to move leave us, barren, we'll move on at
air's bare back,

        akin to sky.

   On another level,

            when day breaks, from the mettle of
this road, its challenge, down to bright stone going slowly
       out not even

           the sensitive hand knows,
surfacing.

Under its heel, broad day, thrown back on the wind's stone paving.

On intangible ground over the road left bare to the light source, every stone lighting up.

Meant for crossing the road before it can be trod down by day dawning.
        As mountain.

        Fire,
                caught every—
                            where ground peaks,
almost reaches me.

ON MOUNTAIN GROUND

Over the Mountains

Today running strong

risk the new day
now plunging into its
cold, white current

hard on
the engine wheeling
out loud

like a knife shifted by air a hair's-breadth

mountains barely lifting clear of ground

if the road wear and break
shift your weight

the roadway is surfaced with snowfall, today.

Fire Where It Shines

Depth here
              whole sea-surge on a field's wing
      takes to the air.

                               Cold, morning light, dazed moth.

Following out day, I've crossed it, the way you cross
tillage.

Stiff with cold

stuff spread

morning as a white
spread

put back together
torn day
that makes up day today

at another pitch

in these frosty wraps

on tilled uplands.

Starting up where the white

                        cold chest is where my line is placed, atop
the wall in one fierce light.

At once wind and body of stone, nib split through which
earth is drawn, rather, at once, withdrawn.

Look, in this huge white blaze boundlessly serving
me as lodging, scant air, air stays bare, and dry.

Unscalable face of air
underneath earth swung up

safely beyond air's inroads

the whole day razed

as a bit of air
in hands held open

mountain

next to nothing

a mountain green
rise to follow
reeling
up.

In Midair

What lapses here answering for breath I lack begins
again to fall like a fall of snow on paper. Night
seeming over deepens. I write as far as you can go
from self.

In Relief

Today the one lamp
speaks out

having taken on savagely
colors it
breaks out and beams
serves up
the last crumb

the white saucer
I can see on the table
rounded by air

the true stone-
cold revives
now

ceaselessly right

out loud pitched

high.

The snow of our breathing melts
solid now

living

slow-paced

as a wooden table

under the crust
of earth's wild glare

live matter
pictured yesterday
by now light shelved

with dry clothes
you shed.

Sealed in place
certain to bloom
all over again

nothing disturbs
the shadow
life of my room

even buckets of cold
sent from atop
an air mountain shape
something like a pail

it quivers
as a lamp will

I light up

I can make out

letters

on this
unpeopled tableland.

Ups And Downs

Around and about, I've turned straying
                     about this shining. Tearing
myself, anew, at the same side of the same day's
wall, torn clothes like air caught about you,
                     the same cold shine.
By now on the other side of the wall I see the same
glare, blinding, dazed.

                  In the distance without a
break and even farther something like the same stretch
of broken ground which, pushing on, I tread, no one to
feel the heat.

Our look will be washed clean out of us, as the air
crowning the wall.

Wind, The Next Wall

At daylight's utmost verge,
                         a breathing, where earth
starts yielding, furthest reach still breathing. I reach
the ground beyond, out of breath, hold, fast,
                              ground here
heaving colder than any road.

Thinning overhead, the farther it gets from the trodden
floor, such ceiling reveals mist another head, wind's,
cold, day breaking, thrusts through.

                       Heat gone the air does not collapse.

On a Sudden the Air

Where, at this wall's foot dark shadows, another dark
waits, cast
      by this sky.

Night, and this nighttime fury,

          white rush of breath

keeping me from my bed.

Wan, vague skyline,

      at a gasp, a breathing space. Echo, I

  set forth through resounding day.

         The house comes to life. Splitting

             the air.

Breakage

Distance is less remote than this sunlit ground, bed and
bite of cold air,

              here where you stop, short, as some
harrow, poised on the red, flaring mould.

I stand, over the green still, in sheer air's daze.

Inroads of earth on us, incessantly bearing in on us,

                   yet I don't remove
from the day.

Nothing,

       otherwise, today, is

              trodden. Undergoing it I

yield to stripped air.

        Over this the stretching

           of road.

UPPER STORY

On The Second Floor

On open ground I emerge, issuing from twigs, from
windows,
    as a house of stone, into air flogging bare
walls of this tasteless dwelling.

Something like, black, near at hand between the two window openings, the wall where I end up. Everything blazes up, rekindling yonder.

I was shored up the while by the room placed at my disposal.

Behind the tree, sky in a white cuticle, and the quick gulp of fiery earth drunk neat by us all. To have twice dived into land around me right up to the skyline. Budding vacancy, this hearth casting no shine, like an open window.

Moving out, relocating the walls bare, bare stone and
this fireplace weariness denies itself as two mere
twigs, dry sticks, mullion and transom, lightless now,

                              the hem of sky, full,
surrounded by woods, on the eroded steeps.

When it comes, earth's second emblazoning, I enter that
overarching white brow which I never notice walking
beside me. This forehead rising over my head, very
height, mighty.

All of a blush right down to the ground. Part heat,
part fireplace, all blaze.

Blaze here comes to a white wing, everywhere that air
blows. Through this gap pierced, skylight.

I pass right through the house image. How to picture
myself reduced to the walls. To the room reaching
wall to wall. Elsewhere fire has drawn in. Earth where
it repairs, into distance, restores.

Like the dead weight of earth its steppes restore.
To be widespread, loosened, lost, scatter our home.

Before us is a mountain, there,

                                bite of

                                       air form

          hung by a thread.

Paper walls taking all light down to faded daylight's
glimmer. Voice with brittle corners. Earth stretched
over you like a hand everywhere sky stands
in for wall, bare lathing level

                    with stones

     underfoot.

Wild ice-cap,
              airless, treeless, tight-fitting over the
roughcast earth, rough guess, sticking as close as you
get to earth itself.

That part, clean and white, where the cloud rack, day-
rent, rips apart, where we're ending up. Knee thrust
against door wood, or this draught of earth neat
                                        coughed up.

Scouting the empty field, these several times, on its
outskirts, I will have, from myself, been sundered, once
more torn clothes.

Such a wall will do to hold evening come. Some few
snatches of breath, whistling against the dark face.

Great stubborn field

heart attack.

It all begins here at this stub of mountain,

headless, left

undone,

lost at a turning of hushed earth.

MOTOR WHITE

The Blank Thrust

I

Quickly having lifted
off a kind of token swathing

I arose once more
freed
anew beyond hope

as kindling
or a stone

I beam

with the same heat as stones

looking cold again
and hard at field
core

yet I bear heat as well as cold

the fiery framework

and fire

whose head
I can see

white limns.

Blazing stitches at several points the dull side of
sky, side I had not ever glimpsed.

Sky lifting barely a bit above the earth and its
soil. Black brow. I do not know that I am here rather
or there,
          in air or a ditch. These are bitten off
clods of air I tread, plodding, earthwards.

My life stops here with this wall or else steps on
and out where the wall ends, at racked sky. I have
no end.

My tale will be the black branch
where it elbows

      sky.

IV

Here opening a white maw, there closing ranks all
along the line, dug in behind these trees, the tall
dark-branched beings, it holds out, only elsewhere
to take on warm, dragging forms of weariness like
shins of earth barked by the plow.

I linger at the edge of my breath, as on a doorsill
listening for its outcry.

Outside, here, there is, on us, some hand set, sea
of weight and cold, as if in kinship we were to join
hands with stones.

I let myself out
into the room as if

already outside

shifting among
furnishings fixed

in warmth quivering

by itself gone out

beyond its fire

there is still nothing
at all

risen wind.

VI

Set in motion, running on fire, with paperthin steps
I pace on, merge in air, over the harmless earth.
I lend my arm to the wind.

Not one step farther than the paper reaches. Very
far ahead of me it fills a gully. Just a bit farther
into the field, here we are almost even. Half-way
to your knees in stones, knees carry you on.

Nearby, pointlessly, talk of a wound, of a tree. Out,
looking out for myself. Not so mad, or so as not
to be. So that my sight may not grow dim as earth
turning earthwards.

The field holds me
much as a water droplet
on red-hot iron

in itself blotted
out is
eclipse

the stones open up

as earthenware stacked
a man
took in his arms

as dusk rises

I stand

with these stiff white plates

as if clasping earth
herself

in my arms.

Already day, spiders spin the light towards me, over
earth in all its particulars. I rise straight over
the tilled field, on waves working, short and dry,

                                    field
the same, finished, turned blue, where I pace on beyond
ease, straining, inelegance.

Nothing will answer. I can answer for nothing. Suffice it
the breath of fire blow, such light flower and fruit both,
enough it fuse with one road grown white, one beam in
eyes of stone struck, sunstroked.

x

I brake to catch a glint of empty feel, is it sky or the
above part of wall. Between air and stone I move into
a field less the walls. I get its skin, the air, at
least, of air, for all that we keep to ourselves.

Outside ourselves there is

no trace of fire.

Almost too near at hand one vast bare page quivering in scorched earth light holds out until once more with one another we close.

Letting it go, the warmed door, its iron clasp, here
I am up against crude noise with no end for the time
being in view, someone's tractor. I reach bottom on
stone, rough sheets I don't begin to tread. I have
always lived. I can see the stones more clearly as
of now, at once the dark grip of shadows and red earth's
dusk over your hand, as it crumbles, beneath its drape,
warmth keeping nothing from us.

Fire, outbound, say a glassy wall drawing out and
upwards the other striking brutally right to the top-
most roofbeams where it binds, dazzlingly blinds, as
a wall without my leave won't go all stone.

To itself true, stern earth raises up its head.

This fire acting as an open hand to which I give up
lending a name. If that of the real has come by now
between us like a wedge, torn us apart, that must be
because I drew too close, to this heat, held to this
flame.

XIV

So then, unutterable vision, such outbursts of wind, great
disks of broken bread, land gone dun, here as it were
hammer-head husked against the current riding
high upstream furrowless where no one makes out more
than the rough bed, open road.

These slivers, these slicing waves set down and forgotten
by wind.

Stones stood on end, grass on its knees. And this too,
what I cannot say, sideways, backwards, be it day from
the moment it is hushed: yourself, as in night.

This you retreats.

Such fire unharnessed, put to rest, yet far from total
exhaustion, flaming us still like a tree, on the slope
along a spell of road.

There remains, after the fire dies, these last stones,
flat rejects, lightless, cold, loose cinder coinage, a
field's change.

And then the splendid carouse, the wash of surf still a
glittering wrack that clashes as if frothing up around
the tree bedded in cold earth nails broke and tore,
whole head lifting clear severe gleams and behest of
silence like a broad field.

Earthbound

Broad earth's full store

tilled gates lifting into yield of air

bounty out of doors

sea-surge

storm's ripe grain

parched

the hub of iron sears

having to wrestle down your own din

bursting land throughout

this thrust I wield

which grows on you

a sudden tree laughs

as the open road burning where my steps vex

as the sun setting skewered on trees

as the wind's red-lunged thrust

here revealed

all I bare anew.

What The Lamp Consumed

Once more as wound reopening

light enough
to read

where we plunge obscure

our dusk
gauged by mountains
shadow height

I started out
with being

this stray twist of wick

earth

fitted to a passing
wind sleeve.

I yield without giving up flame, on fire

on straight

slopes.

Stony. My mouth today opens new, a new
day. Ending the long decline I start afresh.

Like the ceiling you watch high in a mirror, here I
gather up the mountain-cast gleams.

Light lives in the one room's dark portion, where
in the dusky corner the table rises up.

A path here, as a breathlessly rushing stream.
I lend my own breath to the stones. Then I push
on shouldering shadows.

Through our strain we remain aware, wooden
limbs' fuel, bonfire abrupt flame forsakes,
flagging cold where day drops. We take cold.
Then I set my back on those who embrace.

Our scything sweep bestrides the fields. We
speed faster than the roads. Than sight, than
cars. Fast as the cold.

Penetrating countryside. Dwellings. Yet I
don't stop here. I glimpse the path we failed
to take, through the usual face.

Where I see nothing, I get the look of air, grasp
cold by the lugs.

To The Lees

Today's wine wins over
already halfway through

to high noon's
red midland

with a road at the bottom
whose metal belonging
to me wheels in vain

the whole earthen
crock keels over
caves in

come to a stone house

stepped on

and I stop
each time it strikes
pitted stones blind.

Another Venue

The French, thrust as stones from view, translated
twice by the roots from earth, sunk now in walls
which wrap you in their lodging. Bared to the double
fire, pointless and far-fetched, both blunt and over-
precise. I can add nothing to such night nor counter
broad day so focused, so exalted, however taut
stretched, to my uttermost.

One cleft cleaving to what opened is: light treading
about.

Yet I scant thin air hurling down, scarfed about us,
barely wordless,
                            down to flawless battering rain
on walls' pith, to its small wail.

Track down the wind, right to fire's cold glare, down
to where the tree once stood, stark socket, earth unful-
filled, there

       to find yourself standing.

From extremes of sunlight flooding uplands to the drained
lackluster air of this highroad we set our backs to.

Wind, rather fire, really raiment close fitting down to
the heel, stub of day, dark edging the brow.

    Wind full-blown as in the dead of night dawn.

Kept, ourselves, by stone
       walls plastered on all hands
     present shelter from the dark

          vault or is it cave.

Both the blank and the din

daylight exacts my tribute

with naked blade

lighting up
ice-cold glass

bare skylit exactitude

unpictured panel
slate flamed
glacial

flurries on the panes'
deep freeze.

My lodging already half rubble I can see
as a mountain rousting us from the bed
and burden of sleep.

Painstaking relentless loaf, portion without letup
mountainous.

ON THE FACE OF HEAT

Threshing

Haystacked, some other summer's shine. Millstoned. As
the face of earth no one sees.

Setting out again I start over this road doing so
well without me. As giddy firelight embedded in air,
       air eddies over the sunken road. Every-
thing goes out. Already day's sheer heat.

Storm blowing dry-eyed. Lost to view the frosty freeze
breath. Without having set ablaze the litter of strewn
fields.

These four walls, the other storm raging. As cold, cold
as a midsummer wall.

These straws. Whole sheaf. Turned towards one wall of
several summers. Gleam of straw caught in the thick of
summer. Chaff.

So Close to Dawning

Hard by what lights your way,

                        as far beyond its strength
overreaching heat ranges, lapses, already I catch, yet
farther on, the roll of air over dry ground. Where rose
the sun, gripped by dew.

Cleft Lights

Fire gone beforehand into our summer, as one road
tearing every which way. With a storm's chilling
lash.

Such heat. when I guide it out,

                         I have, outside, my-
self, bound wind.

The straw we still lean on, to rest, straws brought
up against the scythe.

From the start I sort out air from road, in summer's
image. Where its cold went, the whole set ablaze, up
in smoke.

★

Through the rent day breaks again, as astounding fire
breaks out. From stones. For you who linger over vistas.
Near, far, same bed, same scything blade, the one wind.

Heat Face

Halting,

        until air itself, lighting up, find me
out here, I stumble on this heat rising flush with
stones' brow.

        Before sky, drying, dry, come
    into its own.

Akin to the air this clear air cleaves, murky
depths of heat.

Embrasure

As a wall our own face, struck by the very same
firelight.
  As cold held hard to a single skyline.

Just brushing, hugging dense ground, the rise
of this knitted brow alongside me.

Another spacing echoing our brow, right across
this excessive heat, just the tiniest bodying
forth of summer.

With a rush it all goes, through water where it
stands, breaths of air.

  The knotted roads freed for us as flame.

It took right to the end of daylight
to come to terms with day.

Today fire burns under another name.

THRESHOLD

Stepping Out

                                 Nothing keeps the road from
merging with accidents of sky.

Pushing on, towards the deep cold stuff of such
sky,
    straw scarcely colder than ourselves, whole
armfuls pile, strewn flare, blaze-broken you must
cross, at the knee which goes
                        into eclipse.

I hold two hands now in mine, strawy hands, straw
both. Near me a brow of straw moves on into the
murky field, beneath this same white knee. Come
between my limbs and my voice,
                        ground, daylight ahead.

Near to a doorway in this one room where lost I
move, is circling skyline.

My eyes opening on air
meet the same air as daylight.

Iron blades' drag travelling back and forth on blunt
stones. The earth, heaving, thunders.

New light, even clearer, stronger, takes our
hands. The gap between us grows even wider as if
sky, where two faces look and lock, in mist with-
drew, hugely, beyond our ken.

Eyesight lives on air's leavings, this drawn look I
scarce make out fades away into the cold of cold
earth, ashes in the mouth.

No sheer brightness outstrips the light of day. No
                                     mere water makes it

     speed.

I look on this vivid air as if up to the smooth sky-
line rail encumbered by the entire spread before
me, spanned. On the new-plowed mould where day evenly
new hangs in the balance, drinks in every step,

                                       frees,

fast in its blank waver caught, ourselves.

As the robe thrown over this icefield time's wear
and tear clothes with its rime.

This inner wall

                  out front coming if unlikely even
closer,

       if our feet know nonetheless to shake off such
dust as clings and grinds them down, like cold clods.
I know as well, on this hearth trod cold parting ever
so slowly with its own heat, that behind me the sun,
one burning ear, turned to me attends, I need not lift
my head towards its ruddy folds before night roll
down, grind us to dust.

As some water droplet hanging, before it falls to
slaking earth.

           I see earth parched.

I come back without
                having ventured out
                                unpacking
earth at its bounds, to these, at
                the evening hour where along just a bit
of edge day still flickers, or runs in a fiery band.
Yet the white cliff,
                gold-glazed,
                                frozen
by light thrown into relief raising a ripple of faint
mountains.

                I go into air as ice sublimes.

Even then, when the whole earthy frame is enflamed, its
thrust day to day spent, flogging itself abroad, as step
by step over the roads' rack,

                more spent than fled or ceased.

Lining, well inside, that wall's open face the wind
sweeps through, well ahead of sight lunging into depth,
a tree, wall, windows lacking,

                                alongside the cold
low road it overspreads,

                something like a door already day
knocked wide open.

                That

                        brilliance,

                                  commanding height dread

                      crown of day.

      The very second its fire caught in air again it
withdraws, faceless, day's utter whiteness wins over the
day without sun.

                        Here, keeping us from the field, such
light, the sloping roadside page.

Keeping on towards this changeless drywall at which
I have always turned myself right about I move pain-
fully up to the utter fixity of the next, the other, wall.

Distant air seizing far-off strongholds leaves us
living things behind.

Leveling

With me I keep a recollection of dewiness over this
road running on without me,

in the helpless wind
risen to meet us.

Sky, in the long vacancy dust shows
where its breath fled.

Spread before me,
even asleep, could it be the same I
find before me, yesterday, breathed in.

The ground acknowledges my every step as the road's own
scrawl in eyesight's hand.

I tarry, at some length, where day stands fast.

Outgoing Flame

The very knot of breath catching,

                above,

                  up with

    bound air, lost.

Riven, disbanded like the riverbed along with the
        rush of water, the above, by

                loftier

      wind.

As in dream to be the river, welcome cold, through
every peopled spot.

From the mountain, this wind, it may be, at dawn end
of day.

Air, spent, duly, done, dazzles, closing over my tread.

Far From Breathing

Having run, without seeing, without acknowledging
it, straight into air, now I can drop towards day.

As a voice, shrinking, at the very lips, dries up
brilliance, or, cold, could.

In the grip, on either hand,
                              of fields outstretched
                    lost to us
              yet up to us, here, reaching.

As heir, I enter on solid ground which rising not
quite to the lips, drinks sun-drenched dawn.

What I walk on shifts not one step out of place,

                              at full stretch grows.

YIELDING

Wind

     risen across dry bygone summer leaves us on a
heaving crest, bare edge, all that

                        of heaven still stands.

Flaw by flaw, accurate earth becomes itself. Set
foursquare like a table earth stands when the blast
strips us.

Here, this world of blue, blue-swept, undisturbed, I have
nearly touched the far wall. The depth of day lies still
ahead. Unsounded, flaming depth of the earth, in depth,
out front, over the face,

                  made plain by one cold
blade, breath, taken.

Brought so far, at the entrance I pause, pulling myself
together as air, blue, where plow turns, furrows meet.

            Nothing will quench my stride.

Translating André du Bouchet

We start with the book—no, the book is already here, in your hands, opened to your gaze and the light of day. To find a starting point we must go back, out, beyond, to where the words start on their way to the author, then to us, then on the next leg of their unending course. The choice words point to a choice of words; the choosing by the author chosen by words to represent them points in turn to the power of words to move—whom, and from where to where moving?—which will make up the matter of the book finally beneath our eyes, in the light of this provenience. Nor must we forget that in translating we have moved, from one language to another, not words—since the original still stands across the gap and since we don't translate words—but the moving and the power translating motion into emotion. That translation is all we can hope to bring over into English.

French words do not move the way English words do. Indeed one of the singularities of André du Bouchet's poetry is its insistence on the motion and power proper to French. To translate that, we must locate and insist on the far different powers of English. On the first page *scythe* stands for the French *faux*; more, *the scythe* must render *la faux*.

The noun is not felt to be feminine in French; the gender, which we can evidently not allude to in our genderless speech, distinguishes *la faux* from its partner and polar opposite, *le faux*. *La faux*, on which André du Bouchet will insist, insists perforce on the masculine word bound to it by the very sweep which carries it so far away. The English scythe will not even allude to *false*, or *fake*, or—to go back to the original Latin—to the notion *deceitful*. In place of what the French declares—that *la faux* is about as far as you can get from *le faux* and its trumpery world, appearances, logical rigor, linked concepts—we must rest content with the hard-and-fast reference, a "feeling" perhaps, whatever inferences we draw from that plus the several "associations" word and object may still help us to: "Father Time," say, who "mows down" the generations of man.

Time is at work as the poet works, as we read; André du Bouchet has taken his stance nearby, within its "reach," without seeming to notice the stuffy old allegory and its grim lessons. The stance is affirmed by the first title, which we might have rendered, "On the scythe's side." His *faux* cuts through, cuts away, all such fakery as Father Time and his cohorts: *la faux* meeting *le faux*. Time was—now gone, back in 1961, the year *Dans la chaleur vacante* appeared—when the scythe, in the French countryside, was still the chosen tool of most men, and women too, daily mowing, reaping, tidying their fields; everyone knew how to beat and hone and wield the blade. Their scythe cuts through history, mythology and folklore too, takes up a lasting everyday incisiveness, baring ancient earth. Soon enough we discover that for André du Bouchet, as for others on other countrysides, the sickle shape of the blade stands daily for the cutting sweep of the horizon, the swing of the sun through the ecliptic, regulating the seasons of sowing and reaping, time itself in its swath.

Soon enough we will meet other curving blades, the plowshare for instance. *Blade* will be rendering *lame,* a thin strip of any material, also the singular ocean wave, its filed crest, onwards thrust and relentless inescapable force. Like *faux, lame* also transcribes into the hard-and-fast domain another of the ghosts haunting French: *l'âme,* usually given as *the soul.* Cutting through its superstitious appeal, *la lame* affirms not only its own bright daytime assertions, but the gap across which it thrusts to make such assertions and others less translatable into words. Soon enough we will meet the brightness of the blade in that gleam through which the dark metal slices, none other than the brilliance of day, the cold shimmer of the air we split as we move ahead hour to hour, none other than the dazzling white of the page where sun treads, across which march in waves the strips of poetry. Without that shine of this day, the dark blade, the dense human figure, the black print, all would disappear, as indeed they do each day at nightfall. Without the gap across which it moves to meet and conjure *l'âme, la lame* too would vanish from our awareness of its peculiar trenchancy.

André du Bouchet begins as I have, with such assertions, highlighting words whose drama is exemplary in his experience. How many words in French follow suit, if less dramatically? So many in that compact language, older and slower moving than our own, have retained less suppleness in function and reference, like our words, than a stiff array of tendencies in perpetual discourse, leading by steps from far right to far left like French assemblies since the Revolution. The French genius for distinctions has, when and if necessary, kept the competing claims apart, tacitly, albeit with a sharpness which never fails to astonish English speakers. Our own tongue, enamored of extention, flexibility and the explicit, has unpacked the portmanteau words, tagged and filed the nuances in a vocabulary several times the size of French. The *faux* or the *lame* can operate through the verb *couper*; but this single term carries all the senses we have labeled *cut in, cut off, cut through, cut down, cut up, cut out, cut into, cut away, cut short,* not to mention *slice* and *sliver, carve, mince, slit, slash, chop, incise* and the rest, not forgetting the colorful *hew, sunder, sever, cleave, rive, hack, split,* for which French might, if need be, find an equivalent even where *couper* would serve.

The most usual of these would be *trancher,* which also means to decide a thorny point, cutting through pros and cons, or else the Gordian knot. And reminding us that words can be trenchant as well as cogent, decisive for speech, thought and action, separating sheep from goats on any occasion where words and occasions are well used. On future occasions indeed André du Bouchet will be exploring an awesome skid his word *faux* takes into deontology. The same Latin root for deceiving which gives us our cluster *fall, fail, fault* will provide French with the twin verbs *falloir* and *faillir*; *il faut* will translate lack, fail, be missing, yet give too the commonest French expression of impersonal necessity, a little like our verbs *want* and *need,* on the model of the Greek *deîn.* Absence, fault or flaw, is curiously what determines us absolutely. What is wanting enjoins. In French, the distinctions we make decide and divide us; in English we blur, confer and concur. André du Bouchet's words insist on the power of words to move and action to speak decisively into the gap crucial words open. *Avancer,* to move on or get ahead, also means to set forth in speech; *poursuivre,* to prosecute a felon or carry on a course of action, means also to pursue a line of argument. All our terms for the brisk march of verse match the motion of feet in space and the progress of words, in song or on the page, within the breath or down the line. Poetry's rhythms are originally those of dance, the foot lifts and falls, *arsis* and *thesis,* arching through the gap of air and treading solid ground, alternately.

Pied makes this point in French, as does *foot* in English. But the trenchant disjunction of rise and fall, accent and pause, blank space and dark print, inhale and exhale, wasted breath and cogent speech, all rhythmically paired, is put in French by the little word *pas.* The word for step, the sonorous junction of the foot and what supports it, *sol* or *souffle,* ground or breath, is also the particle which usually completes the two-part French negation: *ne...pas.* André du Bouchet's *pas* swings violently across the gap, between the arrest, the refusal, the cutting denial of the negative, and the onward thrust of accession. *Pas,* in its terrible dialectic, names the disjunctive basis of speech itself: the brave sweep of sheer motion through thin air, or else—and then—the shock of the all too human foot meeting the all too solid ground.

The gap into which the foot thrusts is, for André du Bouchet's French, no less disjunctive. *Le jour,* the day into which we advance on foot or with speech, in step, pulsing together, beating time, is also an empty opening. *Jour*—light, daylight, daytime or illumination—cannot be discerned without an aperture in stone, flesh, cloth or paper, through which to peer. The *pas* is made or spoken on a trodden *route*; the French word's span has been typically segmented by our triplet, *route, road, rut.* The route the foot takes across fields or a page may follow no known road or else the deep ruts; a route may only be traced after footprints have marked it. In either case the route will have been opened—so says its Latin origin—by someone for the first time, for everyone led to take it.

Le jour and *la route* are no less open this way than *le souffle,* no less a stretch, reach or gap—*un écart*—into which the foot cuts decisively, or stumbles. We can translate wind, breath, breathing, breeze or inspiration—air in motion across hills or through lungs, same air, same motion; thin air, mere noise; or else air laden with dust, dark, rain, or our syllables; the broad sustaining power of our drive or else gimp, endurance, the sustained thrust itself through words into touch with what is not ourselves but sustains us. *Souffle* yields the same range of senses still more or less clearly traversed by our *wind,* plus a few extras on each side carried by the verb *souffler*: to blow, or rest while taking breath, to extinguish, inflate, whisper, prompt. Somewhat the way *lame* disputes *l'âme, souffle* in this poetry gives the lie to another typically French ghost whose goings-on are equally evasive for the translator: *l'esprit,* a word which to my knowledge André du Bouchet has never used unless in this way.

What your feet on their way or your words on the breath find opening ahead is best put by André du Bouchet as *l'éclat,* another term of baffling scope. Splendor, a gleam of something shining, plus the shine which gleams; also an explosion, a burst or outburst; also the shards or splinters of what shone and has, in a gleaming moment, shattered. The word makes points articulated across its span by an action not our own, something like a flash, reaching us in an instant, ourselves instantaneous. The sun's brilliance, source of all we see, comes across—its own dazzle unbearable unless fleetingly—through the medium and on the sights where it breaks into reflections and refractions. Their éclat, for our eyes, mirrors and continues it, bearing out the original. This outcome is named with bare sufficiency by the attribute *blanc,* its anagram almost, a complex notion English breaks down into blank and white. *Blanc* means also unsullied, unfulfilled, inoperative, qualifies the virgin marriage or the sleepless night, the bare page or the open contract. *Carte blanche*, like a blank check, we know, is freedom, to act as one will or must.

And the white available through the gap as *éclat* acts on us as we see and name it. André du Bouchet's titles tell us how. *Chaleur*, white heat of the sun and human warmth as well, is *vacante*—empty, free, vacant like a room, house or office awaiting its next occupant; but also, as the verb *vaquer* suggests, looming up, roving around about its business, at its leisure. *Chaleur* yokes fire's or sun's heat to that of a heated argument or hot chase, with the suffix which everywhere in French indicates an agent, *acteur, facteur, lecteur, auteur*. *Chaleur* is thus the reciprocal of *glacier*, which so often here names the white bulking large out front: glacier, yes, but also the maker of ice, or mirrors...and of ice-cream. The white of *Le moteur blanc*, like the motor, can be noun or else qualifier; *moteur* has held together meanings which English has sifted out into motive, mover and motor. The title swings from a white which is first mover and original motive force, through a blank which is a motivating agent and the freedom to respond, to, finally, a surrealist shocker or a pop art whitewashed diesel. But here, in the book of poetry, we cannot fail to notice that the object of the motive force is in the word itself, is the word itself, the *mot*, made and conveyed by the white it embodies, with ice and heat.

We started out looking, beyond the book in our hands, for beginnings. And we arrive, astonishingly, at the book in our hands: white pages lit by sunlight spread open awaiting our gaze; prosodic feet travelling their route across it, aligned with a known road or not; receptive space going about its business at white heat; dark print starting from the white, generated by it, curling around it letter by letter; the depth of air, light-filled, carrying the page to our eyes, into them and beyond. These are no metaphors, there is only one light, one white, one refraction and one motion, of which the page gives the conspicuous example. The page is continuous with the process and power which inform it. The book is a privileged jurisdiction of persuasive phenomena, undergoing the same surge of the same forces working through matter across time, forces of which we become aware as we partake in them. Writing and reading carry on in their way the breathing, walking, advancing and pursuing of the individual, bearing the motion he embodies. No metaphor because no relation, where the partaking and the embodying are continuous. The book—this one is here to prove it—is as much where we began as where, reaching towards the irresistible source, we begin and will begin again.

At every point, in a book of André du Bouchet, we are led to conclude that the book is of a piece with what bears on and bears off all else. The arts of language like the others, when practiced in probity, do not offer either a counter-world or a counterfeit image of world; but speaking directly for forces which show up elsewhere otherwise, they lead us there. To what coherence and what conclusions are we led by a limited outlay of choice words which as in French seem so outrageously at variance with themselves? What syntax could draw from them a modicum of communicative clarity? French, with its vestigial inflections, its rigid syntactical order, its rigorous system of agreement in number, case and gender, has made of clarity a shibboleth and its legendary pride; while English, marshalling serried ranks of synonyms in loose-limbed marching order, neglects discipline for results, gladly trades syntax for winning tactics, achieves power, precision and persuasion without a second thought for clarity. In English, poetry and prose alike hold out for power and precision; in French, clarity is the ideal of prose, while strict versification, of a complexity unknown to English, has heretofore assured coherence outside clarity or in its despite. What kind of coherence can we expect from French poetry now that the stiff prosodic rules and their analogue, the prosodic world, have wilted? The book, a book of André du Bouchet's such as we have before us, gives a trenchant and a cogent answer to these perplexities.

Incoherence of a telling sort—the single word serves as one of his titles—may be the best and the very best we can expect. The Latin suggests a stutter, the voice stuck fast; but also a persistence, a sticking in. The syntax of each page here, without sticking servilely to the rules, by so much alludes respectfully to them. Incoherence is far from chaos, as is the mesh of forces with which, we concluded, the page and the book cohere. The primary articulation of each word—its first syntax so to speak, if to speak at all—is with the blank which allows it to appear, the gaping gap which parts it from words to right or left, above or below. Words emerge from the speaking not from the speaker, their mouthpiece: language and its speaking support, breath or page, were there before each of us learned to use them. The versification of each page gives the form of respect we give to its economy. Early on, André du Bouchet must have conceived, then stuck to resolutely, a sovereign rule: speak only if spoken to. And its corollary: write only at the first intensity. Each verbal fragment, word, dangling clause or phrase, will be worth recording only if it pronounces on an immediate incandescent experience. Experience of what? we cannot say in advance, experience will dictate, when the word is forced into utterance by imperious articulation, not with other words—in a formula, catchword, commonplace, old saw or venerable idea—but with its singular emergence from the unspoken. Each experience will be a first appropriation, by the speaker, of the word pronouncing on its first occurrence as itself.

Experience, thus, of the unique experience apt to fuse the word with our lips. The fresh formulation of each old word will be the gauge of its authenticity, of its right to recorded utterance, and the sole guide to versification. Each word thus produced, pronounced, appropriated and recorded, bears compounded weight and the force of a complex drama. Each word thus arising from previously unspoken experience—not, that is, from other words—stands out salient, fragmentary and whole both. The experience it registers will be fleeting—a glimmer of a gleam, *éclat* of the original *éclat*, the dazzle of sunlight say, caught and reflected in passing by a bare blade. It coheres syntactically with light and—across a gap of silence fallen where it will be forgone and forgotten—with other words catching similar glimpses of the one light which one by one reveals them all. Since the experience, cutting in, cuts off as we break into speech, then break off again, on the page the stream of utterance cascades in continuous discontinuity. The thrust of the broken lines cannot be seized without a careful gauge of their relation less to each other than to the blanks which join and part them. Over syntax, versification prevails, recalling Homeric paratax and—happily for the translator—the tactics of English, the harmonies and counterpoint of music, the espousal of words and air in song, the musculature of poetry rippling soundless through traditional verse.

The espousal of words and air: who performs the service, who registers the glimpse through words on a breath of air into light? We will not expect to find a familiar voice taking up this task. The old words are fearfully opaque, unless a sudden glimpse through enlighten them and us, revealing uses which such an experience supersedes while as it were commenting on them, fulfilling their promise in an unexpected future. Like the word and the book, the individual is of a piece with the forces which brought him into being and will bring him out again. Exerting or undergoing them, he too remains opaque until enlightened, in each instant superseded, opened to a future. A page is turned, a new voice emerges. Which speaks less for the old, unless to comment on it by implication, than for the new slice of experience, the next glimmer of the irrepressible gleam. Small wonder that the voice of the page bears no more than the brusque accent of the person we thought we knew when we met him on the street, with his panoply of gossip, news, jokes and other faithful standbys which feign a fixed relation to speech and the society it binds. The voice here is shifting, anonymous, disinterested—having long since renounced the convenience of a steadfast self. *Personne* in French names a persistent moral or physical entity with a recognizable face, but also no one, just as *pas* means step onwards and not one step, just as *rien* means a something or else nothing. André du Bouchet's "person" is, in the book, the working face of the page. Its voice, as so often in the older poetry, takes on a function we hate to acknowledge: our habit of miming voices not our own, only our own as we assume them. When we read:

Quickly having lifted
off a kind of token swathing

I arose once more
freed
anew beyond hope

as kindling
or a stone...

we hear the sun speaking of the morning's advent, in which
it is the principal actor and sole author. To our surprise, the
sun's words also give us a man rising to greet the sun; and
that greeting itself, the words arising through the sheets of
bleached linen or white paper or pale mist or blank verse.
The greater surprise is to find these three voices joined, and
registered, in the same words, by a fourth which displays
them with that effortless skill we used to call art. Can we say,
should we ask, which voice may be that of "the author"?
The upshot is to learn that "rise and shine" defines the day
in which a man and the sun and their joint language coa-
lesce. Speech arises where day breaks, divining its source.
The title of this page is, "The Blank Thrust," an alternate
translation of "Le moteur blanc." Sun's rising into its sky
has been translated into words rising to their task from a
man rising to his full height, to catch the first gleam and
make it his own.

Similarly when we read:

> I am fed on fire from stones.
> I deny myself
> there is a hand
> outstretched
> straining
> in midair...

the voice of the page is telling how light and words nourish it, the hand of the translator hovering in the gap between waiting page and expectant gaze. The outcome will read as an effacing of self, in the act of registering light which enters stone, be it the gem, the building- and the stumbling-block, or a mere pebble, revealing and defeating its opacity with the force of a future, today. Nor should we forget, reading these words, that the hesitant hand of another translator has hovered over the French page. The future of the word thus lighted and recorded is also the presumptive future in which, across the gap parting and joining two ancient languages, we may bring over André du Bouchet's voicing into a new English.

However various the voices he assumes, however fragmentary his glimpses into and through his words, an individual will have had the generosity to give us what becomes, in the giving, a coherent vision: earth waking in a dream of earth. The material calling of the book once heeded—meaning and matter locked in a perpetual wrestle, voices twined into a single sounding cord, the white paper double-spread like wings to the light, the motion of feet traversing the turning page, the lines scaling the mountainous height, the in-and-out back-and-forth of words arising from their bed daily, the taking-up and the putting-down by hesitant hands and eager gaze—reverses the incoherence of intermittent glimmers. So that a coherence-in takes over, as the book crosses the gap—in the event, the Atlantic—between writer and reader, between the reader and his future identical for a time, we will hope, with that of the words. Only a single-minded on-rushing future-bent individual could have brought together for us the conditions of this reversal, not a team, system, technique or gambit, in the abeyance of live tradition. That too we must translate, first of all, hardest of all.

The task will be the easier, I've hinted, as the accent of our author, when it appears to approach a personal tone, speaks for language itself, for the onwards bent of any language thrusting into its future and ours. Easier too as André du Bouchet has special bonds with our speech: educated in America between 1940 and 1948 at Amherst and Harvard, he is more deeply versed in English poetry than many writers and readers of English. The result, for readers of this book, will be subtle if unmistakable. I've suggested that his syntax is nearer to a version of English tactics than to the patterns of clear French prose or to traditional versification.

Readers of Henry Vaughan will not be put off by the inner span of his words and constructions, not unrelated to that of the "metaphysical conceit," minus the wit, the irony, the doctrinaire slant of the learning. Readers of Wordsworth will recognize the gleams of intuition in "spots of time," the out-of-doors venue of the inveterate "wanderer," the sense of an overarching "power" training our perceptions, the unremitting progress through encounter, intuition, forgetting, remembering, oblivion. Readers of Gerard Manley Hopkins will not be daunted by the conciseness of diction, the "sprung" rhythms, the collapsed syntax, the ellipses, the rigorous voiding of the commonplace, the willingness to take every risk including that—more an earnest than a risk—of "obscurity." Those who savour the later work of William Carlos Williams know this risk and others boldly taken: the indifference to "style," clipped notation cutting close to the bone of the hard-and-fast, the open reliance on rhythms of speaking and breathing, a laconism devoted to just what punctual gleams shoot askance through broken speech, allowing "the poem" to write itself each time in its own unique guise.

French readers approaching *Dans la chaleur vacante* in 1961 found perhaps less to recognize. The work could be collocated if at all with that of a few solitary figures who took similar risks with equal intrepidity: Maurice Scève, Charles Baudelaire of course, but also the Mallarmé of *Un coup de dés* and, most evidently, Pierre Reverdy. Yet this book—the first to display André du Bouchet's mastery, after several reconnoiterings of the terrain—marked his departure from outright dependence on Reverdy's example, as on that of older contemporaries he had once found occasion to admire: René Char, Francis Ponge, Michel Leiris, Henri Michaux. His acknowledged affinities were with a scattering of independent, sternly original artists: with the painters Pierre Tal Coat and Bram Van Velde, the sculptor Alberto Giacometti, the typographers Guy Lévis Mano and Iliazd, who collaborated on sumptuous illustrated books. Or with the few foreign authors he would take the risk of translating: Joyce, Shakespeare and Hopkins; Pasternak and Mandelstam; Hölderlin and Celan. These appeals to a handful of allies in the past or the plastic arts suggest that André du Bouchet's first important book placed him outside current versions of "literature," already beyond the literary work of his time. Even the loose group of literary friends who gathered around him to found the review *l'Ephémère* would be distanced as the work progressed. Excepting of course the inimitable Paul Celan, so soon to disappear—he who, I must not forget to add, was the first to translate, into German, the book we are now approaching.

Early readers were, to judge by the comments—not by any means hostile—bewildered by the absence of what this poetry was doing very well without. The usual resources and materials of the art seemed to have been cleared away. Gone the lyric emphasis, the elegiac eloquence, the high-falutin' pronouncements on matters of life, love, death. Gone too the intimate avowals, the furniture of sentiment, the décor of suggestive imagery and vivid comparison. Nothing pretty, arch or witty; no description or information, not the slightest hint of a story. No plays on words, no play at all; no meditative posture, no theatrical posture, no posturing at all. This poetry seemed out neither to divert nor to enlighten, to teach, testify or amuse. Seeking the gist of an undertaking so elusive yet so firmly assured, early comments fell back on the language of poverty: André du Bouchet's writing was arid, ascetic, austere; *dépouillé,* bare or barren, remote or hermetic; a solitary pilgrimage towards an inaccessible unknown elsewhere.

Some of the first and many later readers, however, wondered rather at what this poetry was doing with its own wealth of means than at how much it did without. And this view has gradually prevailed. Certain younger men, we have learned since, were struck with *stupeur,* dumbfounded, not so much with delight as with dismay, at language and experience whose severe intelligence did not appear even to allude to old heart-felt concerns and techniques, but stepped beyond them with a single stride, banishing their proud centrality, dwarfing their vaunted stature, reducing contemporary attainments in the art to a closetful of toys. What dismay, what distress, to find André du Bouchet starting from scratch on the far side of where most writers stopped. Mastery had meant pushing the language to the limit of its strengths; André du Bouchet set forth where the language failed. Relieving us of admiration for its triumphs as of a useless burden. A few early readers indeed breathed a sigh of relief, as at a homecoming.

To almost all, André du Bouchet's poetry has spoken in a key not so much new as foreign, the power of the revelation depending on your ear and your courage. Since, with better acquaintance of a sustained creative thrust now spanning 40 years, we can more sanguinely accept as a heritage the "wealth of means" André du Bouchet has found to hand outside the purview of the literary circumscription. What was so strange was to be shown here, irrefutably, that our language simply does not do what we like to think it does—that instead it is tirelessly about a business of which, reading or writing or speaking, we may only get inklings in moments of inattention quickly forgotten, often as quickly as possible. Words' references come daily to hand; words' meanings, forgotten or scanted or hazy, can be checked in the dictionary; words' uses have been mapped and scheduled in grammars; words' functions are the matter of literary commentary and sociological investigation; words' history is the rich domain of the philologist. To words' implications we have no guide; for one reason because they come and go in a twinkling; for another because they spring from each individual context, from each reader's grasp on it or lack thereof; for a third because they cannot be stated using other words without a prompt slippage, a warp, even a caricature.

And yet—here is the wonder—to find these implications solid, patterned, durable, telling, substantial, the very matter of words' true concern; to chart them in their own eery yet curiously native jurisdiction, was to write a "foreign" poetry, to cast again and again on our familiar speech a harsh light. How can we know what we say we do if we don't even know what we say?

Of what I call implications, I found examples at the start, as we set out from the book on the search for beginnings. Among the implications of *la faux* are many which arise in the gap between it and *le faux*. Likewise *pas* and *pas*. What about the implications of *orage*, the storm, revealed by *rage*, madness, pain, anger, but also the rage to live and create? What implications spark from *pierre*, stone or rock, through *paupière*, the eyelid? Or from the obvious concrete fact that the *pierre* can equally be a gem, a building-block, glacial débris, fruitpit or flint? To move into our own language: what kind of bond links *stone* to the one in it? *wall* to the all in it? These are crude self-evident puzzles, which may have nothing to do with semantics or etymology. Or they may: some few words' implications are already well-charted. When André du Bouchet uses *lampe*, he is aware the word "comes from" and reproduces the Greek verb *to shine*; lamp was one term, in earlier poetry, for the sun. When he writes *sol*, soil, ground or floor, he recalls the Latin word for sun, as in our jocular "old Sol." When he titles a poem *l'Inhabité* he remembers that the word in Latin means the opposite of the French. This is not pedantry but practical handling of some telling implications in everyday words. Our language is at one remove from Greek and Latin, the implications arise between languages, between words, within the word itself, whose meanings have been folded loosely over each other, trapping vast hollow reaches where implications echo and clash, rebounding, resounding, compounding a babel we happily shut our ears to. Babel: the Hebrew for *gate of God.*

Our own words are largely obscure to us; most obscure may be their meaning for me today, in the daze of experience which gives them an overwhelming grip on me. I have tried to state this plainly, without recourse to fancy talk, to jargon or to "metaphysics." André du Bouchet's insistence on the imperfect obscurity of our words has been thought to show a "metaphysical" bias. I would wager that few present-day writers are more averse to metaphysics. The coherence of his vision argues, however, a persistent and persistently serious reflection, out of sight here, which we may call "philosophical," though it does not debouch on a "body of thought" much less a philosophy. But rather on a poetry, doggedly pursuing its own line of inventive discovery without a thought for the rhetoric of fashion and party. If our words are obscure, almost any will serve to trace the obscure power to its source. André du Bouchet uses plain words, successively new ones, in the course of his investigations—but so voluminous they no longer resemble the drab

flat ones we have been taught to expect from "plain poetry."
Volumineux: luminous flight. It is both the strenuous atten-
tion and the trusting inattention he brings to bear on them
that illumine their volume, their staggering portent. And
this, as the stagger seems to grant, is their "metaphysical"
bias.

Such an implication seemed to be figured globally, from
the start, by the insistent "blanks" dominating print and page.
But there is no figure; the looming fathomless white of the
page is itself a speaking volume, one with the work of light
everywhere. No silence either, but an expectancy of speech
and silence, where words' cutting in is cut off. The brutally
interrupted lines bring us where words fail—where, in fail-
ing us in our hope of a familiar countenance turned back
towards known speech and its delights—literature, say—the
reading eye is thrust into the gap, you catch your breath,
caught short as the implications arise. Our own words fall-
ing short, going blank, eclipsed at every turn—there is the
substance of the "metaphysical" implication brought home.
What words do not catch and hold, but always reach for and
vainly embrace, coheres incoherently with all the solid back-
ing we trust, including our own mortal matter, to which the
eye is blind, including that of the unseen interlocutor.

The implication, finally, is of that interlocutor, viewless,
the translator translated by his words out of sight. We write
for eyes we do not see. But he and his matter are assured,
once writer or reader places himself at the point where lan-

guage, that of his own time, gathers itself for the leap ahead. For words to carry, into their future and ours, they must have weight. Words swollen with heavy breathing will carry like a party balloon. Words laden with the need to say great things sink quickly from sight. Each word's own gravity must be finely gauged, taken on like a responsibility, then cast onto the page into the balance, about its own task: forging future. To carry, with weight, words must have room to move. Setting forth from the edge of his apprehension, the writer must keep aloof from his own speech, writing as far as he can get from his false identity and its blindnesses, aloof from his presumed reader as well, avoiding equally in relation to words, self and reader the confidential, the off-hand, the trivial and the casual, all too conveniently closing the essential gap. Nothing can be seen when you're up too close; reception and perception, with the momentary and momentous identity of the individuals concerned, suppose an ample circumambience. Familiarity in address or proposition—banter or claptrap—will snuff out the light and stifle the breathing space without which fresh recognition is unthinkable.

Lacking a prosody to guarantee such light, air, amplitude, writer and reader now face freedoms whose challenge few have been prepared to take up. With the flattening of language into a picture screen, its troublesome implications merrily blinked; with the kneading of linguistic variegation into a single doughy pidgin; with the growing hegemony of the technical arts, usurping the ancient rule of the language arts; it would appear that writer and reader were doomed to a closet drama, mouthing astute lines to each other before a coterie of adepts. Surely the bewilderments which greeted *Dans la chaleur vacante* gave ironic expression to a legitimate astonishment: that the poetic endeavor could still be, in good faith, not just possible but imperative. Surely the enthusiasm of bowled-over readers acknowledged the mockery into which writer-reader collaboration had sunk. The risks and rigors of the adventurous intelligence moving a language into its future have ennobled our poetry whenever the density of available speech met that of new implications and dovetailed. Surely the "strangeness" of André du Bouchet's book marked our estrangement from this bequest of isolated yet all the more prized achievement.

Across the gap between writer and reader move discrete packets of experience in a broken order which their own versification assures, quanta of energy which André du Bouchet will call *morceaux,* pieces or morsels, bites or, we might even say, mouthfuls. Words bitten off; portions of a nourishment; precise emotions. Homer and Archilochus were working with similar quanta—it is no surprise to learn that our poet as a youth was a fierce Hellenist. And the Psalmist, Dante and Villon and a constellation of lesser lights, ill-noticed or half-forgotten, across the years still gleaming: Skelton, Belleau, Aubigné, Blaise de Vigenère, Traherne; Blake, Clare, Senancourt, Leopardi, with consummate mastery of tact and taste doing something "way out," dauntlessly and dauntingly strange. The legitimate astonishment is to find a poet taking up that challenge now, for the very first time working, because he must, *against* the drift of his times, braving social and linguistic tendencies which might once have supported, even encouraged, his lonely effort. Proof that language has the resilience to support and encourage him in mid-air, in the absence of all but the rarest reader, the grudging colleague, the hard-pressed translator.

This resilience on which André du Bouchet risks his undertaking has also been the classic resource of the authors I mentioned. It exerts its firmness within the stringent correctness with which each has appropriated the strengths specific to his own time and tongue. That other resilience on which some stake their effort—the ability of a language, notably our English, to slide into easy possession of novelty, stretch if need be thin to take in the current cant, the jazzy idiom grasping gaily at the latest straw of fashion—boasts the correctness of the snapshot and the elasticity of the rubber band. André du Bouchet's plain language is plain French but not exactly the vernacular. On his page, from the taut web of native locution springs a luxury of surprises, leading their own life, which is not like ours but could scarcely be led without it. His correctness plumbs permanent virtualities of written French, a toughness of mind, a passionate restraint at the core of the language—the only sense of *âme* which André du Bouchet would find useful. Or say the grave precision Baudelaire admired in the fastidious poetry of

Sainte-Beuve; the same toughness which tightens the knots of perspicuous irony La Rochefoucauld called *maximes*; which permitted Louise Labé or Marceline Desbordes-Valmore to write with such cool exactitude on frankly emotional ground, which grants Verlaine exquisite control of a vehemence even more heady... Or like the explorers of light—to take up references André du Bouchet would give—Hercule Seghers, Poussin, Cézanne, returning to the spot at a thousand light-filled hours to make with pencil or brush their succinct notations, putting to the test gifts of attentive intelligence and its language rarely united in any art: toughness, delicacy, obstinacy...

The varied strengths of core French can best be appropriated by working in its light, with its grain, maintaining vigilant respect for the proper, in some senses of that broad word we have borrowed from French. Proper speech is "correct" when it draws on the indwelling properties of the language, whose verve gives us access to the intricate literality of the world language constitutes. The book at last before us, modest in aspect, opens a run of ever-bolder ventures in which, advancing at all deliberate speed with seemingly unflagging courage, André du Bouchet has recast, considerably refined and even enlarged French literality. An advance which, in his 72nd year, bids fair to continue. The old self and its old story, gratefully doffed like an ill-fitting threadbare garment, bare to view a flesh and frame at least credible, at best tonic. What version of English is proper to render for now—until the next translation—the proper of these trenchant emotional moments? for we do not translate words, but discrete emotions binding word to world. In their strict adherence to the native hues of a language and thus to its constituent energies, one overarching emotion is found to subtend the rest and guarantee them like a rainbow: jubilation, which goes without saying in the original. Should we hope to translate that too?

DAVID MUS
Dijon, March, 1995

Born of Russian parents in 1924, André du Bouchet grew up in Paris. Upon the Nazi occupation of France, the family fled to the United States, where du Bouchet completed his formal education. He returned to France in 1948, and began translating and writing poetry. By 1961, upon the publication of his first major book, *Dans la chaleur vacante,* du Bouchet had already been recognized as an important poet. In 1986 du Bouchet was awarded the *Grand prix national de poésie* of the French government.

Although he is a strongly independent poet who rarely appears in public, does not teach, and does not write criticism or journalism, du Bouchet has collaborated with many artists; with his colleagues Yves Bonnefoy, Paul Celan, Louis-René Des Forêts, Michel Leiris, and Jacques Dupin, he founded and edited for several years the literary review *L'Ephémère.* Among his books are *Cendre tirant sur le bleu, Qui n'est pas tourné vers nous, Ici en deux,* and *Axiales.*

SUN & MOON CLASSICS

PIERRE ALFERI [France]
Natural Gaits 95 (1-55713-231-3, $10.95)
The Familiar Path of the Fighting Fish [in preparation]

DAVID ANTIN [USA]
Death in Venice: Three Novellas [in preparation]
Selected Poems: 1963–1973 10 (1-55713-058-2, $13.95)

ECE AYHAN [Turkey]
A Blind Cat AND *Orthodoxies* [in preparation]

DJUNA BARNES [USA]
Ann Portuguise [in preperation]
The Antiphon [in preparation]
At the Roots of the Stars: The Short Plays 53 (1-55713-160-0, $12.95)
Biography of Julie von Bartmann [in preparation]
The Book of Repulsive Women 59 (1-55713-173-2, $6.95)
Collected Stories [in preparation]
Interviews 86 (0-940650-37-1, $12.95)
New York 5 (0-940650-99-1, $12.95)
Smoke and Other Early Stories 2 (1-55713-014-0, $9.95)

CHARLES BERNSTEIN [USA]
Content's Dream: Essays 1975–1984 49 (0-940650-56-8, $14.95)
Dark City 48 (1-55713-162-7, $11.95)
Republics of Reality: 1975–1995 [in preparation]
Rough Trades 14 (1-55713-080-9, $10.95)

JENS BJØRNEBOE [Norway]
The Bird Lovers 43 (1-55713-146-5, $9.95)
Semmelweis [in preparation]

ANDRÉ DU BOUCHET [France]
The Indwelling [in preparation]
Today the Day [in preparation]
Where Heat Looms [in preparation]

ANDRÉ BRETON [France]
Arcanum 17 51 (1-55713-170-8, $12.95)
Earthlight 26 (1-55713-095-7, $12.95)

DAVID BROMIGE [b. England/Canada]
The Harbormaster of Hong Kong 32 (1-55713-027-2, $10.95)
My Poetry [in preparation]

MARY BUTTS [England]
Scenes from the Life of Cleopatra 72 (1-55713-140-6, $13.95)

OLIVIER CADIOT [France]
Art Poétique [in preparation]

PAUL CELAN [b. Bukovina/France]
Breathturn 74 (1-55713-218-6, $12.95)

LOUIS-FERDINAND CÉLINE [France]
Dances without Music, without Dancers, without Anything
[in preparation]

CLARK COOLIDGE [USA]
The Crystal Text 99 (1-55713-230-5, $11.95)
Own Face 39 (1-55713-120-1, $10.95)
The Rova Improvisations 34 (1-55713-149-x, $11.95)
Solution Passage: Poems 1978–1981 [in preparation]
This Time We Are One/City in Regard [in preparation]

ROSITA COPIOLI [Italy]
The Blazing Lights of the Sun [in preparation]

RENÉ CREVEL [France]
Are You Crazy? [in preparation]
Babylon [in preparation]
Difficult Death [in preparation]

MILO DE ANGELIS [Italy]
Finite Intuition: Selected Poetry and Prose 65 (1-55713-068-x, $11.95)

HENRI DELUY [France]
Carnal Love [in preparation]

RAY DIPALMA [USA]
The Advance on Messmer [in preparation]
Numbers and Tempers: Selected Early Poems 24
  (1-55713-099-x, $11.95)

TED GREENWALD [USA]
  Going into School that Day [in preparation]
  Licorice Chronicles [in preparation]

BARBARA GUEST [USA]
  Defensive Rapture 30 (1-55713-032-9, $11.95)
  Fair Realism 41 (1-55713-245-3, $10.95)
  Moscow Mansions [in preparation]
  Seeking Air [in preparation]
  Selected Poems [in preparation]

HEVRÉ GUIBERT [France]
  Ghost Image [in preparation]

KNUT HAMSUN [Norway]
  Rosa [in preparation]
  Under the Autumn Star [in preparation]
  Victoria 69 (1-55713-177-5, $10.95)
  Wayfarers 88 (1-55713-211-9, $13.95)
  The Wanderer Plays on Muted Strings [in preparation]
  The Women at the Pump [in preparation]

MARTIN A. HANSEN [Denmark]
  The Liar 111 (1-55713-243-7, $12.95)

THOMAS HARDY [England]
  Jude the Obscure [in preparation]

PAAL-HELGE HAUGEN [Norway]
  Wintering with the Light [in preparation]

MARIANNE HAUSER [b. Alsace-Lorraine/USA]
  The Long and the Short: Selected Stories [in preparation]
  Me & My Mom 36 (1-55713-175-9, $9.95)
  Prince Ishmael 4 (1-55713-039-6, $11.95)

JOHN HAWKES [USA]
  The Owl AND *The Goose on the Grave* 67 (1-55713-194-5, $12.95)

LYN HEJINIAN [USA]
  The Cell 21 (1-55713-021-3, $11.95)
  The Cold of Poetry 42 (1-55713-063-9, $12.95)
  My Life 11 (1-55713-024-8, $9.95)
  Writing Is an Aid to Memory [in preparation]

EMMANUEL HOCQUARD [France]
The Cape of Good Hope [in preparation]

SIGURD HOEL [Norway]
The Road to the World's End 75 (1-55713-210-0, $13.95)

FANNY HOWE [USA]
The Deep North 15 (1-55713-105-8, $9.95)
Radical Love: A Trilogy [in preparation]
Saving History 27 (1-55713-100-7, $12.95)

SUSAN HOWE [USA]
The Europe of Trusts 7 (1-55713-009-4, $10.95)

LAURA (RIDING) JACKSON [USA]
Lives of Wives 71 (1-55713-182-1, $12.95)

HENRY JAMES [USA]
The Awkward Age [in preparation]
What Maisie Knew [in preparation]

LEN JENKIN [USA]
Dark Ride and Other Plays 22 (1-55713-073-6, $13.95)
Careless Love 54 (1-55713-168-6, $9.95)
Pilgrims of the Night: Five Plays [in preparation]

WILHELM JENSEN [Germany]
Gradiva 38 (1-55713-139-2, $13.95)

JEFFREY M. JONES [USA]
The Crazy Plays and Others [in preparation]
J. P. Morgan Saves the Nation 157 (1-55713-256-9, $9.95)
Love Trouble 78 (1-55713-198-8, $9.95)
Night Coil [in preparation]

STEVE KATZ [USA]
Florry of Washington Heights [in preparation]
43 Fictions 18 (1-55713-069-8, $12.95)
Swanny's Ways [in preparation]
Wier & Pouce [in preparation]

ALEXEI KRUCHENYKH [Russia]
Suicide Circus: Selected Poems [in preparation]

THOMAS LA FARGE [USA]
Terror of Earth [in preparation]

GÉRARD DE NERVAL [France]
  Aurelia [in preparation]

VALÈRE NOVARINA [France]
  The Theater of the Ears [in preparation]

CHARLES NORTH [USA]
  New and Selected Poems [in preparation]

TOBY OLSON [USA]
  Dorit in Lesbos [in preparation]
  Utah [in preparation]

MAGGIE O'SULLIVAN [England]
  Palace of Reptiles [in preparation]

SERGEI PARADJANOV [Armenia]
  Seven Visions [in preparation]

ANTONIO PORTA [Italy]
  Metropolis [in preparation]

ANTHONY POWELL [England]
  Afternoon Men [in preparation]
  Agents and Patients [in preparation]
  From a View to a Death [in preparation]
  O, How the Wheel Becomes It! 76 (1-55713-221-6, $10.95)
  Venusburg [in preparation]
  What's Become of Waring [in preparation]

SEXTUS PROPERTIUS [Ancient Rome]
  Charm 89 (1-55713-224-0, $11.95)

RAYMOND QUENEAU [France]
  Children of Clay [in preparation]

CARL RAKOSI [USA]
  Poems 1923–1941 64 (1-55713-185-6, $12.95)

TOM RAWORTH [England]
  Eternal Sections 23 (1-55713-129-5, $9.95)

NORBERTO LUIS ROMERO [Spain]
  The Arrival of Autumn in Constantinople [in preparation]

AMELIA ROSSELLI [Italy]
  War Variations [in preparation]

JEROME ROTHENBERG [USA]
  Gematria 45 (1-55713-097-3, $11.95)

SEVERO SARDUY [Cuba]
  From Cuba with a Song 52 (1-55713-158-9, $10.95)

ALBERTO SAVINIO [Italy]
  Selected Stories [in preparation]

LESLIE SCALAPINO [USA]
  Defoe 46 (1-55713-163-5, $14.95)

ARTHUR SCHNITZLER [Austria]
  Dream Story 6 (1-55713-081-7, $11.95)
  Lieutenant Gustl 37 (1-55713-176-7, $9.95)

GILBERT SORRENTINO [USA]
  The Orangery 91 (1-55713-225-9, $10.95)

ADRIANO SPATOLA [Italy]
  Collected Poetry [in preparation]

GERTRUDE STEIN [USA]
  How to Write 83 (1-55713-204-6, $12.95)
  Mrs. Reynolds 1 (1-55713-016-7, $13.95)
  Stanzas in Meditation 44 (1-55713-169-4, $11.95)
  Tender Buttons 8 (1-55713-093-0, $9.95)
  To Do [in preparation]
  Winning His Way and Other Poems [in preparation]

GIUSEPPE STEINER [Italy]
  Drawn States of Mind 63 (1-55713-171-6, $8.95)

ROBERT STEINER [USA]
  Bathers [in preparation]
  The Catastrophe [in preparation]

JOHN STEPPLING [USA]
  Sea of Cortez and Other Plays [in preparation]

STIJN STREUVELS [Belgium/Flanders]
  The Flaxfield 3 1-55713-050-7, $11.95)

ITALO SVEVO [Italy]
  As a Man Grows Older 25 (1-55713-128-7, $12.95)

JOHN TAGGART [USA]
  Crosses [in preparation]
  Loop 150 (1-55713-012-4, $11.95)

FIONA TEMPLETON [Scotland]
  Delirium of Dreams [in preparation]

SUSANA THÉNON [Argentina]
  distancias / distances 40 (1-55713-153-8, $10.95)

JALAL TOUFIC [Lebanon]
  Over-Sensitivity [in preparation]

TCHICAYA U TAM'SI [The Congo]
  The Belly [in preparation]

PAUL VAN OSTAIJEN [Belgium/Flanders]
  The First Book of Schmoll [in preparation]

CARL VAN VECHTEN [USA]
  Parties 31 (1-55713-029-9, $13.95)
  Peter Whiffle [in preparation]

TARJEI VESAAS [Norway]
  The Great Cycle [in preparation]
  The Ice Palace 16 (1-55713-094-9, $11.95)

KEITH WALDROP [USA]
  The House Seen from Nowhere [in preparation]
  Light While There Is Light: An American History 33
    (1-55713-136-8, $13.95)

WENDY WALKER [USA]
  The Sea-Rabbit or, The Artist of Life 57 (1-55713-001-9, $12.95)
  The Secret Service 20 (1-55713-084-1, $13.95)
  Stories Out of Omarie 58 (1-55713-172-4, $12.95)

BARRETT WATTEN [USA]
  Frame (1971–1991) [in preparation]

MAC WELLMAN [USA]
  The Land Beyond the Forest: Dracula AND *Swoop* 112
    (1-55713-228-3, $12.95)
  The Land of Fog and Whistles: Selected Plays [in preparation]
  Two Plays: A Murder of Crows AND *The Hyacinth Macaw* 62
    (1-55713-197-X, $11.95)